A NEW CLASS

Jarrett J. Krosoczka

SCHOLASTIC

For Joaquin, Mateo, and Jaiden

This book wouldn't have happened if it weren't for the dedication by the following people: Thank you to Michael P., Rick, Sam, Debra, and the entire team at Scholastic shepherding this along and entrusting me with the lightsaber. Much love to Michael : Jennifer, and the entire team at Lucasfilm for allowing me the honor to play aroun a galaxy far, far away. Thank you to Jeffrey Brown for being so kind and graci to me as I carry on this series. Thanks go to Joey Weiser and Michele Chidester their help in shading the interior of this book, and to Austin Gifford for his assist in the studio. And for their patience and love, Gina, Zoe, and Lucy Krosoczka.

SCHOLASTIC CHILDREN'S BOOKS
AN IMPRINT OF SCHOLASTIC LTD
EUSTON HOUSE, 24 EVERSHOLT STREET, LONDON, NW1 1DB, UK
REGISTERED OFFICE: WESTFIELD ROAD, SOUTHAM, WARWICKSHIRE, CV47 0RA
SCHOLASTIC AND ASSOCIATED LOGOS ARE TRADEMARKS AND/OR
REGISTERED TRADEMARKS OF SCHOLASTIC INC.

FIRST PUBLISHED IN THE US BY SCHOLASTIC INC, 2016
FIRST PUBLISHED IN THE UK BY SCHOLASTIC LTD, 2016
THIS PAPERBACK EDITION PUBLISHED BY SCHOLASTIC LTD, 2017

ISBN 978 1407 18195 0

A CIP CATALOGUE RECORD FOR THIS BOOK
IS AVAILABLE FROM THE BRITISH LIBRARY.

PRINTED BY CPI GROUP (UK) LTD, CROYDON, CR0 4YY
PAPERS USED BY SCHOLASTIC CHILDREN'S BOOKS ARE MADE
FROM WOOD GROWN IN SUSTAINABLE FORESTS.

3 5 7 9 10 8 6 4

WWW.STARWARS.COM
WWW.SCHOLASTIC.CO.UK

A long time ago in a galaxy far, far away....

Victor Starspeeder, protector of peace and justice and stuff, stood at the ready. Forces of the dark side were upon him, and he was prepared for battle!

One of the best Jedi, like, ever to exist, Victor easily destroyed the evil droids with his sweet Jedi skills!

So fearless! So brave! He used the Force like a boss!

Jedi from across the galaxy marveled at how Victor wielded a lightsaber!

TO: The parents/guardians
of Victor Starspeeder
RE: JEDI ACADEMY

The guidance counselor at Obroa-skai brought Victor's file to my attention. His natural ability to harness the Force is most impressive. Not many younglings Victor's age yield such power, and we feel that he needs a course of study that will help him harness these talents. Therefore, we are transferring him to the Coruscant campus for this coming school year.

Victor's teachers gave him high praise, and while they state that they are "really, really, really just so sorry to see him go," we are all in agreement that the Jedi Academy at Coruscant will offer Victor the more . . . active lifestyle he seems to need.

Please fill out the attached paperwork and be sure to sign the permissions. I'm sure that his sister, Christina, will be delighted to have him as a classmate. And while transferring into the school halfway through the academic year could prove a challenging transition, I am confident that Christina will help Victor through.

May the Force be with you,

Hexaday

Hello, Journal. If you are from the future, and you're reading this, I'm keeping this diary so you can have a record of how I became the famous Jedi that you now know. And it all starts here. Today is the day I am heading to the Jedi Academy! I can't believe it. Sure, I was at the Jedi Academy at Obroa-skai. But research?! C'mon! I want to learn about cool things, like lightsabers and opening doors with the Force and stuff. My mom said she has a "bad feeling about this," but Mom always worries. She's been a super-nervous kind of mom ever since my dad died, before I could even walk. I miss Dad, even though I never really knew him. But I know he'd be so proud to see me studying at the Jedi Temple! Just like he did!

My dad was the best!

Dad kept journals while he was at school, at least that's what I overheard Mom saying once. She doesn't like to talk about Dad, but I overhear everything that's said around the house and she said something once about his journals being in the Jedi Temple archives or something. (But if you're reading this, it means I became a famous Jedi whose journals ended up in the archives, too!) Anyhoo, back to Mom. She thinks I'll take an eye out with a lightsaber. But when the day comes that I need to save the galaxy and protect my family, will I want to reach for an encyclopedia or a lightsaber?

I wonder what color my lightsaber will be!

My clothes will flap in the wind like this

Me as an awesome Jedi

Books for weight lifting

Yeah . . . I didn't exactly fit in at Obroa-skai . . .

I seriously thought the plants just needed a little air.

So reshelving the books using the Force wasn't a good move . . .

Librarian Buried Under a Mountain of Books, Padawan Responsible

Padawn Stuck in a Tree

I was just trying to help my buddy Jacob avoid a puddle, using the Force.

But I did all right with grades . . . even though the classes were super boring. I mean, the classwork was really easy. I think they just wanted to get rid of me. But, whatever, now I'm on my way to becoming a REAL Jedi!

Look after your brother, please.

Mom! He'll cramp my style!

Help me, Christina. He's a bright kid. He just needs some guidance. We can't have him walking down the wrong path.

Um, you guys do know I can hear everything you say? I'm right here.

Mom, don't worry! You've taught me everything I need to know about avoiding the dark side. I want to be a Jedi Knight, not a Sith Lord!

Monoday

Naboo was barely in the rearview mirror when Christina handed me this note.

> Okay, little brother, let's get one thing straight—at Jedi Academy, you don't know me, and I don't know you. Don't try and pull any of the stunts you did back home. Master Yoda won't tolerate that for a second.

BEWARE OF THE DORK SIDE!

I'm pretty sure my sister knows how to breathe fire.

Oh man! This is going to be so much fun! I can't wait to learn how to do flips and high jumps!

When do we get our lightsabers? I'm gonna be all "VVVVMMM! VVVVMMMM!"

And Jedi mind tricks! I can't wait to learn how to do Jedi mind tricks.

You will clean my room, sis. YOU WILL CLEAN MY ROOM!

Here. Why don't you read the school paper.

The Padawan Observer

EDITED BY THE STUDENTS OF JEDI ACADEMY Vol. MXV #6

VACATION ENDS, SECOND SEMESTER STARTS

We hope that everybody enjoyed their midyear break! We had a great first half of the year, and the second half will be even greater! The faculty cannot wait to get you back into their classrooms! P-10 and the droid team have been working throughout the break to make sure that the facilities are in tip-top shape! Head chef Gary Jettster has been designing a menu that will expand your taste buds with culinary treats from around the galaxy! You might think that Mr. Zefyr would rather you all stayed home, but even he's excited to be back! (He knows that somebody needs to teach young Padawans the art of using a lightsaber properly.) Enthusiastic, Master Yoda is, to continue to dispense his vast knowledge of the Force! Upon arrival, please report immediately to your bunks for your dorm meetings! Let's finish out the year with a bang!

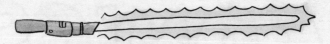

WE'RE EXCITED TO INTRODUCE A NEW FEATURE FROM OUR NEW GUIDANCE COUNSELOR, MS. ARIA CATARA!

ASK MS. CATARA!

Dear Ms. Catara,

I'm excited to get back to Jedi Academy, but I hear that I am getting a roommate. All last semester, I had the room to myself. It was great! But now I'm a bit nervous. What if he snores? What if he has stinky feet? What if he plays his music loudly?

Holding My Nose in Alderaan.

Dear Holding Yours Nose in Alderaan,

The basis for a good friendship iza open conversation and honesty. But howza you tell him his feet are a stinky without making him a sad? That is a toughie! But you know what would make him a more sad? Youza telling your friends that his feet are a stinky behind his back! Maybe suggest he make an appointment with a the school nurse and then theyza can give him some powder! Sleeping with a gas mask for the year won't a be comfortable! And if he snores and plays his music a too loudly? Same advice—has a open conversation!

XO, Ms. Catara

COMICS

WOOKIEE CIRCUS

"Raoooorrr! Raor."

SPOT THE DROIDRENCES!

HUTTFIELD

YOUNGLINGS

GALAXY FEED

12 Facts About the X-Wing Starfighter You Won't Believe!

MUST SEE! Ewoks Dressed as Jedi Will Make You LOL!

What to Do When You See a Rancor... (Spoiler Alert) RUN!

Monoday

After a journey at lightspeed, our ship finally approached Coruscant. I was relieved because I had read the entire newspaper and just about every Galaxy Feed article I could find. And I'm pretty sure Christina was starting to lose her patience with me.

If you don't sit still, I'm going to glue you to your seat.

I couldn't get over just how cool Coruscant was, and we hadn't even landed yet. The repulsorlift traffic was unlike anything I had ever seen before. There were passenger ships and air taxis zipping in every imaginable direction. There were zillions of skyscrapers spread across the land and in a way that was crazier than I had imagined. Everything was pretty tranquil back on Naboo. Coruscant was the complete opposite of that and I LOVED it! My heart nearly beat out of my chest when the Jedi Temple came into sight! This was really happening!!!

Monoday (continued)

When I was leaving Obroa-skai, Mrs. Rondeau told me that I had been a big fish in a small pond, but when I got to Coruscant I'd be a little fish in a big pond. I didn't know what she was saying. Did Jedi have the ability to grow gills? But then I realized what she meant. This place was HUGE and I was like a tiny guppy.

I was taking it all in when I heard heavy breathing behind me. It was like this, "Fitcccchhhh kwahhhh! Fitchhhh kwahhhh." Then I felt a chill in the air. A bone-chilling kind of chill. I started thinking about everything Mom had warned me about the dark side and how people can feel cold when they are near Sith. I started to panic. Were there Padawans studying to become Jedi just so that they could become Sith?! My heart began to race. What if they knew about my dad's heroism and targeted me? The sound got closer and closer.

"FITTTCCCHHH KWAHHHHH! FITCHHHHHH KWAHHHH!" I spun around . . .

Pant
Pant

Excuse me.

Whoa. That kid just brushed me aside using the Force.

And he's carrying his luggage using the Force, just like my big sister . . . but this kid is my age!

It's worth a try.

My underwear!!!

You must be the new kid, Christina's little brother.

Oh man, people already know that? I'll never be cool.

You're cool with me. I'm Zach. I remember my first time here at Jedi Academy.

C'mon, I'll show you to your dorm. Let's go, guys . . .

Monoday (continued)

I made my first friend! Zach isn't just the coolest kid at Jedi Academy, but possibly the coolest of all the Jedi period. He can already do all of the awesome Jedi tricks, like jumping really high and flipping through the air. And he used the Jedi mind trick on the cafeteria staff to score us some free cookies. Free cookies! We didn't even have to pay! And it was super-nice of him to show me to my dorm. He didn't have to do that. He did all of those nice things for me even though he knows my sister is Christina.

Unfortunately, I may have also made my first enemy today. I'm pretty sure that kid in the dark robes is a Sith. It was totally rude of him to push me out of his way using the Force. It's like, man, what is that guy's problem?!

DIAGRAM OF AN AWESOME JEDI

helpful

friendly

DIAGRAM OF A NASTY SITH

brooding

dark robes

cold air

impatient

Here you are, Victor.

Hi! I'm Coleman.

This is Emmett.

Hi.

I'm Victor. I think this is my bunk.

Oh, cool! You're the new kid! They must have assigned you to this dorm because you love the arts, too? I'm pumped for Drama Club this year . . .

Monoday

Christina didn't give me a heads-up on how weird Master Yoda would be. I'd heard so much about Yoda this and Yoda that when I eavesdropped on Christina's holocalls with her friends, and she only talked about how amazing he was. He's supposed to be one of the best teachers at the school, one of the most powerful Jedi! But he was more yadda, yadda, yadda than Yoda the Jedi Master. Nothing he said even made any sense. Coleman told me that I would get used to it. I don't know. I expected him to be taller. And less hairy. But I guess that's what happens when you get old. My grandpa has hair growing out of his ears, and he's only sixty years old. Yoda is like six HUNDRED years old or something like that.

Yoda

My grandpa

MEET THE FACULTY OF JEDI ACADEMY

Principal Mar
Science, Philosophy

Master Yoda

Mr. Cooke
Math, History

Kitmum
Physical Education

Mr. Zefyr
Lightsabers, Defense

Librarian Lackbar
Literature, Art

RW-22
Student Advisor

T-3PO
Tutor

Aria Catara
School Counselor

P-10
Maintenance

Gary Jettster
Head Chef

Student Name: Victor Starspeeder
Level: Padawan
Semester: Two
Homeroom: Master Yoda

CLASS SCHEDULE

0730-0850: PRINCIPLES OF THE FORCE
Master Yoda will lecture on various aspects of the Force and Philosophy.

0900-0950: LIGHTSABER DUELING
Mr. Zefyr will teach students to respect the lightsaber in his self-defense class.

1000-1050: PHYSICAL EDUCATION
Kitmum will lead students through traditional Jedi training exercises.

1100-1150: BIOLOGY OF NONHUMAN SPECIES
Principal Mar will teach students about known life-forms throughout the galaxy.

1200-1250: LUNCH BREAK

1300-1350: USING THE FORCE 101
Master Yoda will continue to train students in using the Force to lift bigger and bigger things.

1400-1450: LITERATURE FROM ACROSS THE GALAXY
Librarian Lackbar will explore the various writing styles of authors from a diverse selection of systems.

1500-1550: MATHEMATICS AND PHYSICS
Mr. Cooke will teach the students math equations governing the laws of physics, as well as how to overcome those laws.

Okay, that was pretty cool. But I thought that we'd be doing something a little more exciting by now.

Who is that?!

Master Starspeeder, present you shall be! Here in my classroom, your body is, but in the stars, your mind travels. The heart can cloud the mind, young Padawan. Open to page ten, you will. And aloud, read!

Duoday

That girl from Master Yoda's class? Her name is Maya, and she is beautiful! And she's super smart. The good news: We have all the same classes together. The bad news: She doesn't pay any attention to me. It's like I don't even exist!

I tried drawing her some pictures and giving them to her in class, but I couldn't get her to take them. Unfortunately, Mr. Zefyr was paying attention and he wanted to see the paper I was passing around.

I froze. I would be toast if Mr. Zefyr saw my drawing! He is as scary as Christina warned! I quickly switched the drawings in my notebook and gave him a drawing of a rancor instead.

Do you want her to notice you or not? Sometimes if you want somebody to like you, you just need to completely change who you are.

Well, my mom told me that if people didn't like me for who I am that was their problem, not mine.

And you're going to listen to your mom? HA!

BRRRING!

There's the bell! Gotta get to gym class.

Triday

I think that Christina must be jealous that I'm talking to cool, older kids, because she handed me this note in the hallway.

Stay away from Zach. He's trouble. And he doesn't know what he's talking about. Also, you've been walking around school with toilet paper stuck to your boot all day.

So embarrassing. She was right! Why didn't anyone tell me?! I'm sure Zach would have told me if he noticed—he's my best friend here. I'm taping Christina's note in my journal so that we can look back at it and see just how wrong she was about Zach.

47

Quadday

Soooooo . . . that didn't quite work out as planned. The droid that got banged up was P-10. His primary function is to fix things around Jedi Academy. And everybody really loves that ol' hunk of junk. I didn't mean to toss the ball so hard, I SWEAR! I have no idea what happened. I don't normally play sports . . . or use the Force, apparently, so I wasn't expecting the ball to go berserk like that. These sorts of things always seem to happen to me. I thought it was such a good idea at the time. Everybody was mad at me. And what's worse is that Maya was all sympathetic to Artemis. I mean, I'm sorry that he got banged up, but Maya was all goo-goo ga-ga over him.

Doesn't she know he's a Sith-in-training?!

I visited P-10 in the repair shop to let him know just how sorry I was. When I got there, Master Yoda was there, too. "Help to fix this, you will." I've tinkered with some starship model sets back home, but never a full-on droid.

Not at all intimidating having Yoda watch me

Me hoping to not make a mistake

Bee ba beep boop!

I told P-10 I was sorry for all of the trouble, and he seemed to really appreciate that.

Once P-10 was all fixed, Zach showed up. I don't think P-10 cares much for Zach, because he got very aggressive. "BEE! BEE! BEEP!" I'm not fluent in droid-speak, but I'm pretty sure he was saying something about Zach and my sister. I dunno. It didn't make sense; maybe his wires were still crossed.

ZAP!

After the incident at gym, I was so nervous about the next lunch . . .

Man, who am I going to sit with?

Hey, Victor!

We saved you a seat!

Hey, Emmett! Coleman!

Uh, hey, Artemis. Sorry about what happened back in gym class . . .

Victor, my man! Come and sit with us!

Whoa! Really? With the older kids?

Bee ba BEEE!

Oh, hey, P-10!

Ooops! I missed the trash can.

Looks like you'll need to serve your primary function, droid!

C'mon, Victor!

Everyone, this is Victor! Victor—everyone! This is Victor's first semester, and he's my new favorite student.

Victor, you ever been in a food fight?

Uh, no . . .

Lemme see your sandwich. Watch this!

This must stop immediately!

SPLAT!

The Padawan Observer

EDITED BY THE STUDENTS OF JEDI ACADEMY   Vol. MXV #7

FIRST-YEAR TRANSFER PADAWAN WREAKS HAVOC IN CAFETERIA!

One Padawan sure knows how to make an entrance. First-year student Victor Starspeeder, younger brother of ace student Christina Starspeeder, started a food fight that ended with Mr. Zefyr taking a dessert to the face. Witnesses to the account report that Starspeeder threw a sandwich that led to the bedlam in the lunchroom. This Padawn will need to learn how to control his feelings as his use of the Force nearly destroyed the cafeteria.

Because of these actions, new restrictions are in place for students' lunchtime. Eating times have been reduced by five minutes, and Padawans are expected to remain in their seats until the bell rings.

Head Chef Gary Jettster on the disaster in the dining room: "It'll take at least a week to get the smell of blue milk out of this place!" More on Page 2.

ASK MS. CATARA!

Dear Ms. Catara,

How do you get your crush to crush back? It seems like however hard I try, she doesn't care for me. And I only end up making a fool of myself.

Help me, Ms. Catara! You're my only hope!

—The Lame-O Padawan

Dearza Lame-O,

Youza tryin' too hard! You says so youzself! Youza should be you! If it waza meant to be, she willa notice.

Hang in there!

XO, Ms. Catara

WOOKIEE CIRCUS

"Groawwwwr!"

SPOT THE DROIDRENCES!

HUTTFIELD

BOOT!

IT'S THE SIMPLE THINGS.

GALAXY FEED

5 Surefire Jedi Mind Tricks to Get Yourself Out of Trouble and Improve Your Grades!

Always wave your hand in front of your superior, and try these expressions!

1. These aren't the Ds you're looking for.
2. You said the paper was due next week!
3. I did, not do not, there is no try!
4. The Loth-cat ate my homework.
5. It wasn't me.

If these fail to work, just blame your droid!

Pentaday

Oh dear, Journal . . . this is not going as planned. Back at Obroa-skai I was one of the most popular kids. But now I am one of the most disliked students! Everyone is mad at me because of all of the new rules placed on lunchtime in the cafeteria. How do I let everybody know that I didn't start the food fight?! If I speak up, I'll get Zach's friend in trouble, and then I will lose the one friend I actually have here. So here I am at the guidance counselor's office, waiting for my appointment. I guess that's one thing that hasn't changed with the new school. Me in an office talking about my feelings.

Is it a requirement that all guidance counselor offices have ridiculous posters hung on the walls? How was this supposed to inspire me?

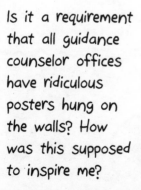

When a yous gets in troubles, how does it a make a yous feels?

Meeza hates to see yous getting into so much troubles. Youza needs to focus! Youza a smart Padawan! A powerful Jedi-in-training!

Thesea three strikes, meez afraid.

Three strikes?! I only count two!

Youza caused damage to a school droid and the food fight, yes . . .

But there's this! Mr. Zefyr found this drawing on his desk. You drew it, right?

How did that . . . ?

I gave this to Zach. Did he drop it somewhere?

Worry not about how your art made it to Mr. Zefyr.

Disrespect our mentors, we will not! Disrespect leads to insolence! Insolence leads to anarchy! Anarchy leads to the dark side!

Hee hee. Captured Zefyr's likeness, young Padawn did. Talent this boy has.

Follow me, you will.

Where is he taking me? A dungeon? Is he going to feed me to a Sarlaac? I'd feed me to a Sarlaac . . .

Neither of those places, young Padawan.

To the theater, we go. Drama Club, you will join! Learn to control your anger, you will! Hmmm? Successfully manage their emotions, a good Jedi must. Learn box-step and jazz hands . . . hee hee . . . young Padawan will!

Greetings, I am T-3PO, human-cyborg relations. I am fluent in six million forms of communication—and I am the faculty advisor for Drama Club.

BEEE-BEE E-BEEEee

Oh, you are so dramatic, RW!

Bee-ba-BEEE!

Yes, I know that is the point of Drama Club.

Oh, all right, all right. This is RW-22, my co-director.

Beeee!

May the Force be with you, young Starspeeder!

Victor? What are you doing here?

Joining Drama Club, I guess.

You're going to love it! Drama Club is so much fun!

Hey, Emmett and Coleman, we're about to begin . . .

You're totally right, Coleman. This is going to be awesome. Oh, hi, Maya!

Victor, you're signing up for Drama Club?

Oh yeah. I'm a huge fan of theater.

What's your favorite show?

Hexaday

I'll be honest here, Journal. I was not excited about Drama Club. Zach told me how lame it was, so I thought I was absolutely doomed when Yoda made me sign up. But then I saw that Maya was there, and I thought to myself, "This can't be all bad." If Zach was wrong about Drama Club, he was definitely right about something else—if I wanted to impress Maya, I needed to be something I wasn't. And a theater kid was something that I wasn't. So I fronted like I had acting in my blood. She grilled me on my favorite shows. I think my answer won her over. Pretty slick, I know!

66

I had these visions of sharing the spotlight with Maya on stage. Maybe there would even be a scene where we got to kiss! At first I wasn't sure about acting, but I could see myself getting used to the whole leading-man thing!

But just my luck—auditions already happened before the semester break! T-3PO informed me that I was on set crew. What?! Apparently this was all Yoda's idea. I have to design, build, and paint all of the backgrounds for the different scenes. On the night of the show, my big job is to move the set pieces off and on the stage between scenes. It sounds like a big job, even bigger because I'm the only member of the set crew! Coleman assured me it would be a cinch, because the set crew just uses the Force. Okay, I thought. But that requires me being an ace at using the Force!!! What if I crush the actors on stage?!

Talents, you have! The spotlight for you, I do not foresee. Paint fake trees, you will! Hee hee!

The Padawan Observer

ANNOUNCING THE ANNUAL MUSICAL!

It's that time of year again! Time for the annual school musical! This year the Drama Club is staging a performance of the classic hit—*My Fair L8-E*! A story about a Jedi and her droid, and the power of friendship to cut through the barrier of man vs. machine! Anticipation will be high. How could Drama Club ever top last year's epic performance of *A Starship Is Born?*

If you're interested in helping sell tickets, please see Maya, president of the Drama Club!

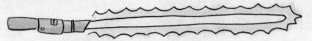

ASK MS. CATARA!

Dear Ms. Catara,

I think my bunkmate might be a Sith. They wear dark robes, they're super mysterious and it's always really chilly when I'm around them. How do I handle this?

Signed,
Sleepless in the Bunks

Dearza Sleepless in the Bunks,

Youza shouldn't judge a book by its cover, or how they sets the thermostat. Iza this classmate bullying you or somebody else? If so, tells a teacher right away! But if not, they might justa be expressing themselves with dark robes. Youza all becoming teenagers soon, and sometimes you'll just gets moody. And that's A-OK.

XO, Ms. Catara

SPOT THE DROIDRENCES!

YOUNGLINGS

COME ON, CHABA-DOWN! KICK THE METEOR BALL!

I HOPE THIS DROID DOESN'T TRICK ME AGAIN.

AAUGH!

METEOR BALLS ARE HEAVY!

70

Triday

I was getting ready to fall asleep when Yoda sent an interesting holomail to everyone's datapads.

Greetings! The big semester project is here. Study one planet across disciplines, we will. A field trip, we will attend. You will pack your own lunch. Hee hee. This year, Endor we will study. I will assign partners in class. Work closely with your peers, a young Jedi must! Good training this will be.

I was really excited. I'd never been to Endor. And just as I was getting amped up, Artemis had to say something from the top bunk.

Technically speaking, Endor is a moon.

Artemis didn't talk much, but when he did, did he need to be such a downer?

I know Yoda is the most powerful Jedi, but maybe, just maybe, I could use the Jedi mind trick on him this one time.

Pair me with Maya, you will.

Hee hee. Cute, you are. For effort, an A you get.

But let's be real here—I don't even know how to use the Jedi mind trick to get extra cookies at lunch. Hopefully, Maya and I could at least spend some time together on Endor. She'd think I was really cool if she got to know the real me!

I'll save you!

All around you, feel the Force. Train yourself to ignore your surroundings. Slowly and calmly, breathe in . . . and breathe out.

I shouldn't have slept in and missed breakfast.

RUMBLE

Young Starspeeder, on our field trip, many snacks should you pack. Hmmm?

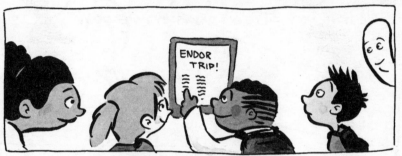

Quadday

My study buddy is a Sith. Well, at least I suspect he's a Sith. I know one thing for sure, he is going to be a total drag. He takes studying super seriously. He reserved a table in the library for us. We each got books on Endor and sat to read. After a few minutes, I couldn't help but notice Artemis was laser-focused. I needed to get up and stretch.

We have very different styles in note-taking.

Artemis's notes

my notes

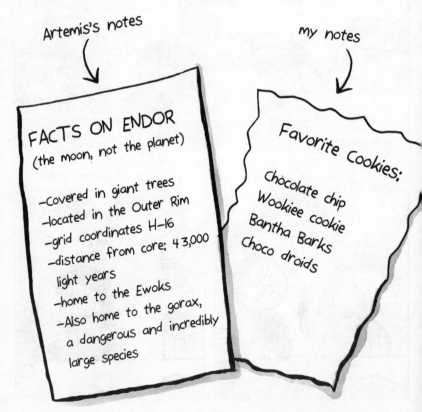

FACTS ON ENDOR
(the moon, not the planet)

-Covered in giant trees
-located in the Outer Rim
-grid coordinates H-16
-distance from core: 43,000 light years
-home to the Ewoks
-Also home to the gorax, a dangerous and incredibly large species

Favorite Cookies:

Chocolate chip
Wookiee cookie
Bantha Barks
Choco droids

Do you want to take a break and run down to the cafeteria?

We just started.

You're not hungry?

We just ate lunch. Did you read that book on plant life on Endor?

It's kind of boring. There are hardly any pictures. And when I press on the pages it doesn't talk to me.

Can't we just look up holos on Endor?

Huh. Power cell died.

These don't need power cells.

78

Hexaday

Hello, Journal. The trip to Endor finally arrived, and everyone in my bunk was flying together. I had packed two backpacks filled with extra robes, but Yoda made me put one back. I guess everyone is okay with re-wearing stinky robes.

Only gone for two days, the kitchen sink, we need not!

I don't know what he meant. I wasn't packing the kitchen sink. Why would anyone bring a sink on vacation? Before we boarded the ship to Endor, Zach stopped me to ask if I could bring him back a souvenir. I told him that Endor was a pretty natural sorta place, and that I didn't think that they had a gift shop. But he said he wasn't talking about getting a key chain or anything like that. He wanted a wish plant. He said they could be found growing in the wild on Endor. Zach said it would mean a lot to him if I could help him out. I figured it was the least I could do, so I told him I would try. He said I'd need a speeder bike, but I've never ridden one before. Can't be too hard, right?

Do you have any Jedi Masters of Spades?

Go Colo Fish!

HA! HA! HA!

Hey, Maya, do you think someday you might want to . . .

We are now approaching our final descent to Endor! Please make sure your seat belts are fastened . . .

Gotta get back to my seat.

85

WHOOOSH!

SWIPE!

BIZ-SHOOO!

Monoday

Okay, Journal, I have a lot of work to do. I know I thought Artemis could have been a Sith, but a Sith wouldn't go out of their way to save their study buddy like that. (Especially a study buddy who does none of the work . . .) And I thought I'd be all tough and brave when I needed to, but man, when I was faced with that gorax, I just FROZE! Like a Popsicle!

I had no idea what to do! And there was Artemis—a kid who I thought was kind of a drag—saving my hide! I want to be an incredibly awesome Jedi Knight! Artemis is clearly on the path to being just that. I never thought I'd say this—but maybe I need to be more like Artemis?

91

Quadday

I received this message in my holomail.
It couldn't be good . . .

93

Pentaday

About five hours into our journey home, Christina started grilling me. She was weirded out that I was so quiet on the trip. "You usually don't stop running your mouth!" she said. I tried to play it off like it was no big deal. But she wouldn't stop asking questions.

You're my brother. I know you better than anyone and I can read you like a book!

So I told her everything. What was up with my grades and that meeting with Yoda, Ms. Catara, and Mr. Zefyr. I told Christina Mr. Zefyr was out to get me. She said, no, he was just out to get good grades from me. Either way, she told me she was going to tutor me over spring break. Ms. Catara told me that she had called Obroa-skai, and that they wouldn't take me back. I told Christina they hated me. She said that a Jedi didn't waste their time with that emotion. "Hate leads to terrible things," she said. My sister is smart.

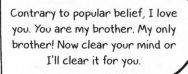

Contrary to popular belief, I love you. You are my brother. My only brother! Now clear your mind or I'll clear it for you.

Plus, I can't have you fail. A Jedi is about helping others, and there's no one more important to help than family.

Is this about Zach? Are you jealous that I'm hanging out with an older kid?

Using the Force takes total concentration, Victor. Like this.

Zach is a jerk. He asked me to the dance last year and I said no. If it isn't obvious, he's using you to get closer to me. Now . . .

Your training, has begun! Hmmm?!

BOOF!

I did it! Huh. No candy.

Dad would be proud.

Do you think?

I know.

But he died when you were just in preschool.

True. But Mom always told us about what a hard worker he was. And brave, too.

So, Victor, did you get all of your homework done over break?

Yup! I even made a diorama of Endor for extra credit!

Great!

Another delicious meal, Russell! And that cake was great!

Thanks! Chocolate Mustafar cake! My specialty!

May I have seconds?

Victor, remember, only one dessert. You need to watch your health!

Monoday

When we got back to Jedi Academy, it was like Christina flipped a switch. As soon as we landed, she was all about her friends and wouldn't give me the time of day.

But she did punch me in the shoulder, which was her way of letting me know she cared. I mean, she really cared! Dad would be really proud of her. I know I'm proud of her. She's super smart, and man, she's going to be a super incredible Jedi someday! (Christina, if you ever find my journal and read what I just wrote, I didn't mean any of it. I still think you have bantha breath!)

Breath mint?

I was amped to get back to school and really show everyone what I was capable of. I know I have the power to succeed. If Christina can believe in me, I can believe in me!

Artemis! How was your vacation?

Adequate. Just the amount of time to be home in Cloud City. The altitudes do a number on my asthma.

I have a surprise for you . . .

Ta-da!

Most impressive!

The Padawan Observer

EDITED BY THE STUDENTS OF JEDI ACADEMY Vol. MXV #9

ARE YOU PREPARED FOR FINALS?

It's the last stretch of the school year! Are you ready for final exams? They will be here before you know it, so you'd better cozy up to a protocol droid and get to studying! And you'll want to get as much academic work in as possible so that you can enjoy two of the biggest end-of-year events—the school musical and the big dance! All of this can be stressful, so be sure to drop in to Ms. Aria Catara's office if you are feeling overwhelmed! A stressed-out Jedi won't do the galaxy any good!

WHAT DID YOU DO OVER SPRING BREAK?

"I memorized all of my lines for the big show!" —Maya

"I caught a lot of great plays here on Coruscant." —Zach

"HA! Vacation? There is no such thing." —Mr. Zefyr

WOOKIEE CIRCUS

"Rwoar Rwoaaaaar!"

SPOT THE DROIDRENCES!

HUTTFIELD

MUNCH!
MUNCH!

SLEEP EATING IS MY HIDDEN TALENT.

YOUNGLINGS

In a galaxy far, far away. . . .

INSPIRATION IS A FUTILE ENDEAVOR.

Primeday

T-3PO is getting really nervous about the musical. Rehearsals have been getting pretty tense. Most of us kids just want to hang out and talk after a long day of classes, but there is a tight rehearsal schedule. T-3PO kept blowing a fuse—both figuratively and literally.

All of the sets have been built, but the painting isn't done yet. T-3PO keeps riding me to paint the very top of the set pieces. He's afraid it will ruin the illusion if the wood is showing. I've also been practicing pushing the sets in and out of place. I have a lot of work to do in that department. And a lot of harnessing of the Force to gather if I'm going to pull this thing off by myself!

Quadday

Painting sets is hard work. There are a bunch of scenes where the characters are walking around a downtown area, and the scene calls for brick buildings. I used a sponge, dipped it into red paint, and padded it on cardboard to make the facades look like brick walls. I probably should have done all of this before the sets were actually constructed . . . it would have been far easier to do this on the ground! Now I needed to get about 12 meters up to paint the top parts of the fake buildings. I tried using the Force to lift up my brushes when I was painting trees, but that saw varying levels of success . . .

But that was also just brushstrokes, this was more precise, and I wasn't that good with the Force yet. So a good, old-fashioned ladder it was . . . It's when I was up on the ladder that the worst possible thing happened. I swear, absolutely swear that this wasn't my fault, but as far as anyone was concerned, I was caught red-handed! Literally.

Pentaday

Just when things were finally looking up with Maya, the paint incident had to happen! I swear on my father's journal that I didn't do that on purpose— or at all! I didn't even think it was funny. Nobody would believe me when I said it wasn't my doing. But I have an idea of who it might be . . . I heard somebody laughing after the whole thing went down, and it sounded just like Zach. I didn't see Zach, but I'd recognize that laugh anywhere. I would say that I can't believe that Zach would frame me like this, but then again maybe I shouldn't be so surprised. It seems like every time that I get into trouble he's had something to do with it. But why would he want to mess with my sets for the musical? Or Maya's costume? She worked really hard on that costume, and now it's ruined! And since she thinks this is all my fault, my chances of taking her to the dance have been ruined, too.

I wrote an apology letter just the same. I'd do anything to make this up to Maya. I went to her locker to hand-deliver my note.

Who is she talking to?

So you'd want to go to the show with me?

Of course! I've never seen a real show on Broadsky before. That is the real deal! Professional actors and everything! I didn't realize you were into musical theater.

ZACH?!

I practically grew up with musical theater.

I just never joined Drama Club because it was too hard to fit in with all of my academics, you know?

Bee-ba-Beeeeeee!

You're right, P-10. I don't want to come across as a snoop. But I don't trust Zach!

I gotta run to class, but I'll see you soon!

Quick! Hide!

Bee-be-baaaeeeeee!

Yeah, I know you told me so!

Monoday

I opened my locker to find this note from Christina:

> Victor! I know that seeing your crush
> hold hands with Zach is driving you
> crazy, but you need to focus! You
> need to pass these exams. Nobody
> is worth you getting kicked out of
> Jedi Academy. I told you Zach was
> bad news. And if Maya doesn't like
> you—guess what? She doesn't like you!
> Move on. Somebody will like you for
> YOU! And if she falls for a guy like
> Zach? Blech!

What can I say? Christina was right. I didn't come
to this school to fall in love. I came to learn. And
to become a super awesome Jedi knight. The big
presentation for the semester project on Endor was
coming up. Artemis and I worked so hard on the
project. I just hope that our presentation doesn't hit
any glitches.

And that . . . is our project on Endor.

Most impressive, this was.

The diorama is just so charming!

Praise aside, they have depicted a member of the Panshee tribe wearing garments that are from the Gondula tribe . . .

Work hard, you did. This partnership bore many fruits. Including an A on this semester project.

Told you.

Plaudits you received. But remember—conceit leads to failure, young Padawans. A Jedi must always keep his mind grounded.

He's just so funny! We just laugh and laugh . . . And it's so cool to talk to somebody who just gets theater, you know?

Yeah. How cool to find somebody who is both funny and appreciates theater. I mean, where else would you find that . . .

That's great, Maya, but can we get back to studying?

Aretmis is right, we need to stay on course. Does anybody have notes from Mr. Cooke's history class?

Hold on, I have some here.

beep beep

Hee hee!

What's so funny?

Duoday

Maya just kept pushing my buttons, and I couldn't help it. I got so mad. The planet doesn't revolve around her. But still, I didn't get a handle on my emotions, and there were books and datapads everywhere. I thought Artemis, Coleman, and Emmett were going to be totally mad at me. Their notes were scattered all across the library. But they actually helped me pick up the mess. Maya stormed out of the study group. I seriously was not jealous! Except for maybe a little. But that wasn't the point. The point was that we were there to study for final exams, and we weren't going to be able to focus with her holopad constantly beeping with messages from Zach.

That little incident at the library landed me back in the counselor's office.

Well, okay, maybe Mr. Zefyr wasn't that harsh. Sure felt like it, though. Yoda told me that if I slipped up one more time, he would have no choice but to send me home from Jedi Academy early. I needed to stay on track and study. I didn't want to go home to Naboo and lead an ordinary life. I want, no I NEED to become a Jedi like my dad. It's the only way I can honor his legacy! Yoda reminded me that Obroa-skai wouldn't have me back. I figured it was just because they hated me. But Yoda insisted that wasn't the case. Apparently my counselor at Obroa-skai knew I would get the best possible education for my talents at Coruscant. Yoda said they really saw potential in me, and they couldn't give me what I needed there.

So powerful in the Force, young Starspeeder is. Have the resources to teach you, Obroa-skai did not. At the Jedi Temple, lies your only option for a path to being a Jedi Knight. Strong and handsome Jedi will you be!**

**Okay, so I made that last line up.

I have to lock up the library, Victor. Sorry! You've been here so often, you'll do just fine on your exams!

Thanks again for helping me, Artemis.

Focus, Victor.

Breathe in through your nose. Breathe out through your mouth.

Triday

It's the night before final exams, and I can't sleep. I've worked harder than I've ever worked before, but I don't think I've gotten anywhere. I'm totally gonna fail these tests. I'd study more right now, but my brain can't handle any more information. At least I'll be able to say that I had one fun year at the Jedi Temple. I made some great friends, and maybe we'll even stay in touch after I head back to Naboo.

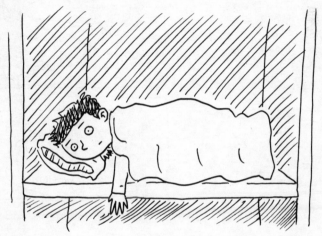

I tried looking at articles on my datapad, but that didn't help me fall asleep. It only ever seems to get me all riled up. Maybe it's the glow of the screen? Or the endless clicks . . . so I broke out the comics sections from old school papers. That helped me drift off to sleep. Not because the comics were boring, but reading printed comics is somehow comforting for me.

GALAXY FEED

Yoda's Throwback Thursday Will Give You All the Feels

Astromech Hacks That You Can't Live Without!

You'll Never Believe What Awesome Thing Happened After This Young Padawan Became a Jedi!

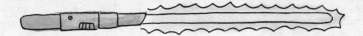

WOOKIEE CIRCUS

SPOT THE DROIDRENCES!

"Rwoaaaaar!"

HUTTFIELD

HEY, HUTTFIELD! WANNA TRY OUT THIS NEW SKATEBOARD?

I DON'T DO EXTREME SPORTS. UNLESS YOU COUNT EATING.

NOM NOM NOM

YOUNGLINGS

TWELVE PARSECS.

FLIGHT ADVICE 5¢

THE DROID IS IN

THAT'S WHAT I DREAM OF MAKING THE KESSEL RUN IN.

IT'S GOOD TO HAVE DREAMS, BUT THAT IS UNREASONABLE, YOU CUBE FACE!

128

Okay, class, there will be no talking from henceforth. May the Force be with you!

Ironic that this is a history test because I'm about to be history...

My mind is getting clouded from anxiety. I can't focus on a single question!

Breathe through my nose, exhale through my mouth.

Okay, Starspeeder, let's see what you've got!

I'm ready!

FWOOOM!

KSCHHH! KSCHHH!

PEW! PEW!

PEW! PEW!

KSCHHH! KSCHHH!

PEW! PEW!

KSCHHH! KSCHHH!

SZHOOOM!

VRAP!

Impressive. But you failed to put the safety lock on your lightsaber when returning it to your belt. Emmett, you're next!

Excellent work, Artemis. An A is your destiny! Victor Starspeeder, next you are! Lift these boulders . . . without crushing school property . . . you must.

Clear your mind . . . a Jedi must!

He's doing it!

Shhhh!

CRASH!

Uh-oh! Look!

x

WHOOOSH!

Regain control, you did.

Under dire circumstances, they were. Hmmmm. Most impressive, young Padawan. Most impressive indeed!

Hexaday

Final exams are now behind me, but I'm sure I flunked them all. Mr. Zefyr must be so happy that he can give me a failing grade. I'm getting ready to say all of my good-byes at the dance tonight. At least I'll have one last hoorah before I head back to Naboo. Maybe I can end things on a positive note with Maya. It didn't work out, but I don't want there to be bad blood between us.

I'm really going to miss this place. Christina was right when she said Jedi Academy wasn't like what you saw in the holopictures. It was so much more than that and so much better, too. Sure, our training sabers wouldn't cut through steel beams or anything. But that didn't matter. I wouldn't trust any of these kids yet with "laser swords," not even with the super-smart kids like Artemis. We'll have the rest of our lives to deal with real lightsabers. Well, my friends will at least . . .

My friends must be around here somewhere.

What?!

Betrayed by my best friend! I knew I shouldn't have trusted Artemis! Only a Sith would slow dance with his best friend's crush!

Hey, Victor!

I hope you guys are happy together!

What happened to Zach? Did you break his heart, too?

I don't think Zach has a heart to break. He didn't turn out to be who I thought he was. When he didn't notice I was there, he was really mean to people. That's not cool.

And I'm not choosing Zach or Artemis—or you. I'm choosing myself. I don't need to go steady with anyone. And I never broke your heart, Victor. Your perception of me broke your heart.

Whoa. That was deep.

Friends?

Friends!

C'mon! Let's dance, I love this song!

Guess what?! I PASSED!

REPORT CARD

Student Name: Victor Starspeeder
Level: Padawan
Semester: Two

JEDI ACADEMY · CORUSCANT CAMPUS

CLASS	NOTES	GRADES
PRINCIPLES OF THE FORCE	Much potential met	A-
LIGHTSABER DUELING	More training will benefit	B-
PHYSICAL EDUCATION		😐
BIOLOGY OF NONHUMAN SPECIES	Quick Learner	B
USING THE FORCE 101	POWERFUL TALENT	B+
LITERATURE FROM ACROSS THE GALAXY	A bit more focus needed	C+
MATHEMATICS AND PHYSICS	a little more application...	B-

Monoday

I couldn't believe it! Neither could Mr. Zefyr. He told me that he'd keep an eye on me just the same. I think I accidentally offended him . . .

> I'll be keeping my eye on you!

> But you don't have one to spare.

Okay, I __know__ I accidentally offended him. Why do I do that?! Sometimes it's hard to stop my inner monologue from becoming my external monologue. Mr. Zefyr was not pleased. But he didn't punish me. I think he's probably running out of ways to reprimand me. I'm sure he'll spend the entire summer break coming up with creative ways.

> Yes, I would like for you to organize my socks by level of stinkiness.

Well, yeah . . . okay. But who they date is their choice—and neither chose you!

Well, this lightsaber is about to choose YOU!

VOOOM!

This isn't what our training sabers are for, Zach. Chill out!

You were supposed to be my tool to getting a girlfriend!

BEE-ba-BEEE!

Yes, P-10, I know he was using me!

145

JEDI ACADEMY DRAMA CLUB PRESENTS:

MY FaiR L8-E

The 294th annual Jedi Academy Drama Club performance!

We'd like to thank our sponsors:

A1 Speeder Repair
Darren's Droid Services
Honest Yarg's Droid Emporium
New Republic Bank
Zelcomm Tower

Program cover by Victor Starspeeder

My Fair L8-E

Cast:

Penelope Doodle	Maya Phoenix
L8-E	Emmett Maxfield
Mrs. Huggins	Lonnie Ashfield
Professor Hoverford	Coleman Flytrap
Mrs. Mak-Mak	Eliza Shee
Mr. Mak-Mak	Shane Brashoo
Butler	Albert Creo

Chorus:
Alessandra Enervin
Hoosha Tookoo
Kyra Jorda
Jalaila Linlee
Villa Yar

Set design and set crew:
Victor Starspeeder

Lighting:
Artemis Oophanoe

WHOOOSH!

Heptaday

The show was a hit! Everybody loved it! Maya was such a great singer! Coleman was hysterical! You know, when Yoda forced me to join Drama Club, I thought it was the worst thing that could possibly happen to me. It turns out, that I made the best friends ever. I was looking for friends in all the wrong places. I was looking in places that just weren't ME! For your very best friends, you really don't need to look too far—you just need to get to know the people that are right there in front of you, in the places where you already feel comfortable being YOU! And I guess that I never had a place where I was comfortable being me before! I loved the challenge of building those sets—and moving them between scenes! When I first got to this school, I could barely use the Force to move my luggage. My counselor at Obroa-skai was right. I didn't belong there. I belonged here. I'm kind of, sort of really sad that the year is ending. I know, I know, I'll have next school year to look forward to.

Hey! Our performance of <u>My Fair L8-E</u> made it to Galaxy Feed!!!

GALAXY FEED

7 Facts About the <u>My Fair L8-E</u> Production at Jedi Academy!

What kind of droid would be your soulmate? Take the quiz!

What should Jedi Academy's Drama Club perform next year? Vote here!

The Padawan Observer

EDITED BY THE STUDENTS OF JEDI ACADEMY Vol. MXV #10

STANDING OVATION FOR A GREAT YEAR!

Another great school year at Jedi Academy is behind us. So many highlights to fit into our time capsules! Who could forget the epic performance of *My Fair L8-E* by the Drama Club this year? Or the annual dance where line dancing was all the rage? What will you be leaving in your time capsule?

(Continued on page 3.)

STAR STUDENT IS LEAVING JEDI ACADEMY

Zachary O'Halleran, a popular Padawan, was just days away from graduating when he disappeared from campus with no explanation. Master Yoda assured *The Padawan Observer* that while Zach would not be graduating with his class, he would be continuing his education. Zach had always expressed an interest in politics and when Master Yoda was asked if Zach went on to Senate School, he simply replied, "Did he? Did he not? The future will tell, I will tell not!"

WOOKIEE CIRCUS

"Rwoar? RWOAR!"

SPOT THE DROIDRENCES!

HUTTFIELD

BURP!

WELL, I CAN CROSS THAT OFF MY ITINERARY.

YOUNGLINGS

I JUST WANT TO FLY A KITE . . .

BUT EVERY SINGLE TIME . . .

THE KITE-THIEVING JAWAS TAKE IT.

UTINNI!

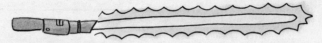

ASK MS. CATARA!

Dear Ms. Catara,

I'm really going to miss my friends over the break. I don't have friends on my home planet who get me like my friends here do. I know I'm not supposed to say this, but I'm not looking forward to summer vacation! How do I cope?

Signed,
Sad in the Summer

Dearza Sad in the Summer,

We do make a special friends when we are here at the Jedi Academy because weeza surrounded by people who understand us. It can be frustrating to the young Padawans to be asked to do silly tricks by their non-Force-sensitive friends from their home planets. Just a know that youza be asked to uzea the Force to get the holoremote and other simple things around the house. And whileza you wait to return, send holos and maybe plan a Padawan playdate?

XO,
Ms. Catara

The Padawan Observer End-of-the-Year Awards

Most Improved	Most Mysterious	Best Dancer

Best Old Guy	Most Chill	Most Stressed

Most Helpful	Best Listener	Best Sense of Humor

Wisest	Growliest	Most Invaluable

Bye, everyone! I hope that you have a great summer!

You, too, Victor!

BEEE!

We're going to be holding a virtual book club this summer. Want to join?

Yeah, every week we'll read a different book then meet in a holochat to talk about it.

Will the books have pictures?

He'd love to join you! Victor, hurry up! We're going to miss our ride!

Jarrett J. Krosoczka is a two-time winner of the Children's Choice Book Award for the Third to Fourth Grade Book of the Year, an Eisner award nominee, and is the author and/or illustrator of more than thirty books for young readers. His work includes several picture books, the Lunch Lady graphic novels, and Platypus Police Squad middle-grade novel series. Jarrett has given two TED Talks, both of which have been curated to the main page of TED.com and have collectively accrued more than two million views online. He is also the host of The Book Report with JJK on SiriusXM's Kids Place Live, a weekly segment celebrating books, authors, and reading.

Jarrett lives in Western Massachusetts with his wife and children, and their pugs, Ralph and Frank.